The Autumn Calf

BY **Jill Haukos**

ILLUSTRATED BY **Joyce Mihran Turley**

TAYLOR TRADE PUBLISHING

Lanham • Boulder • New York • London

Published by
Taylor Trade Publishing
An imprint of The Rowman & Littlefield
Publishing Group, Inc.
4501 Forbes Boulevard, Suite 200, Lanham,
Maryland 20706
www.rowman.com

Unit A, Whitacre Mews, 26-34 Stannary Street,
London, SE11 4AB

Distributed by NATIONAL BOOK
NETWORK

Library of Congress Cataloging-in-Publication
Data Available

ISBN 978-1-63076-237-7 (cloth)
ISBN 978-1-63076-238-4 (electronic)

Printed in Malaysia.

About the Long Term Ecological Research (LTER) Network

The LTER Network is a large-scale program supported by the National Science Foundation. It consists of 25 ecological research projects, each of which is focused on a different ecosystem. The goals of the LTER Network are:

Understanding: To understand a diverse array of ecosystems at multiple spatial and temporal scales.

Synthesis: To create general knowledge through long-term, interdisciplinary research, synthesis of information, and development of theory.

Information: To inform the LTER and broader scientific community by creating well designed and well documented databases.

Legacies: To create a legacy of well designed and documented long-term observations, experiments, and archives of samples and specimens for future generations.

Education: To promote training, teaching, and learning about long-term ecological research and the Earth's ecosystems, and to educate a new generation of scientists.

Outreach: To reach out to the broader scientific community, natural resource managers, policymakers, and the general public by providing decision support, information, recommendations, and the knowledge and capability to address complex environmental challenges.

Acknowledgments

I would like to thank all of the teachers and students who have visited Konza Prairie to learn about the tallgrass ecosystem, especially those of the USD 383 Manhattan/Ogden and USD 475 Fort Riley/Junction City school districts. Your love and dedication to this amazing area is inspiring.

This material is based upon work supported by the National Science Foundation under grant no. DEB 1346857. Any opinions, findings, and conclusions or recommendations expressed in this material are those of the author and do not necessarily reflect the view of the National Science Foundation.

Dedication

Dedicated to Dave and Katie Haukos for their love, support, and constant inspiration; and to Barb Haukos for suggesting the title. —JH

For Rick, my partner in travel, adventure, and life — who enthusiastically supports every outdoor opportunity inspired by my projects! — JMT

When the little calf was born, the days were getting shorter.

Maximilian Sunflower

Maximilian sunflower blooms in the autumn, forming a 6- to 10-foot-tall spire of bright yellow flowers. This beautiful prairie plant was named for the naturalist Prince Maximilian of Germany, who led an expedition through the western United States in the 1830s. Goldfinches and monarch butterflies love these flowers. Monarch butterflies look for nectar in the flowers as they migrate down to Mexico in the late summer. Goldfinches look for seeds, which are very nutritious to other forms of wildlife, too.

Upland Sandpiper

Sandpipers are birds typically found along the shores of lakes or oceans. The upland sandpiper is unusual because it lives on the grassy prairie, where there are no shorelines for miles. This bird is easily identified by its height (it can be 12 inches tall) and its habit of standing on fence posts. From their perch, upland sandpipers scan the horizon for intruders and maybe look for a grasshopper or two for lunch.

The upland sandpipers were done nesting in the prairie and had already left on their migration south.

When the little calf was born, the Maximilian sunflowers of autumn were blooming and cool breezes were blowing from the north.

Tallgrass Species

The grasses of the tallgrass prairie are indeed tall; the dominant grass, big bluestem, can reach over 9 feet by September. The other kinds of tall grasses that make up the "big four" are little bluestem, Indiangrass, and switchgrass. Each spring the grasses' green sprouts grow from the rich soil. Their massive root systems reach down and out for up to 9 feet. Even when you can't see any growth above ground, the huge root system is healthy and active underground. It has been estimated that more than 75 percent of these grasses live below the soil.

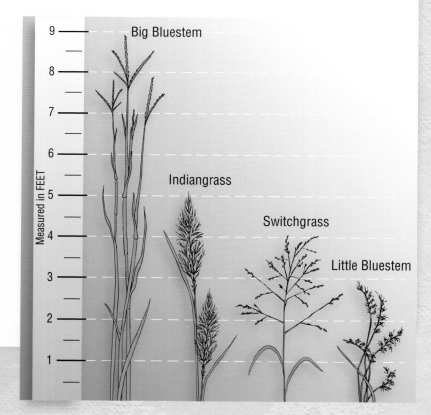

In the bison herd at Konza Prairie, the little calf stood out. She was bright orange. The other calves' orange "baby" coats had already been replaced by a denser, warmer brown coat. She alone still had the orange coloration of a baby bison.

The grasses growing on the Konza Prairie were starting to reach their tallest height. In some places, the grass was taller than the autumn calf, but it tickled the bellies of the older bison calves that had been born in April.

Jill worked at Konza Prairie, where the bison lived. She directed the education program and trained volunteers to teach visitors about the prairie. Part of Jill's job was to know what was happening with the bison so she could share that news.

When Jill first saw the little calf in September, she was surprised and then alarmed. Mid-spring is the normal time of the year for bison calves to be born, not late August. Even though the little calf was a normal bison baby, Jill worried that such a small calf born so late in the season might not live very long.

Winter can be harsh in the Flint Hills of Kansas. The first snowflakes typically fall by November 1, although it is not unusual for snow to be on the ground in mid-October.

The little calf was in a race, and all of the other calves born earlier in the year were already four months ahead of her. She was racing the calendar to gain enough weight and grow a coat dense enough so she could survive the winter.

Wild Bison Can't Be Herded!

Bison are wild animals. They can seem gentle, friendly, and very much like cattle, but they are different. Cowboys on horses are well-known for their skill at rounding up and herding cattle, moving them to wherever they need to go. Bison, however, can't be moved by cowboys. At Konza Prairie, the bison are brought into the corral every year toward the end of October to be weighed and vaccinated. The most effective way to move wild bison is to bribe them! Herd workers go out in trucks to the bison area a couple of weeks before the roundup and give them treats while they honk their horns.

The bison soon learn that when they hear the honking horns, treats are coming. On roundup day, workers drive toward the corral while honking their horns and the bison simply follow them.

Gene, the bison herd manager at Konza Prairie, kept a close eye on her. His experience told him that the little calf would need to weigh at least 200 pounds by roundup if she was going to survive.

The older calves were already experimenting with eating grass, even though they were getting milk from their mothers. They were growing big and strong and would easily live through the winter. Our little calf had not had enough time to learn how to eat grass yet. All of her food still came from her mother's milk. Gene knew that the little calf had a smart mother, and he hoped the mother's knowledge and experience would be enough to help the calf survive the winter so she could eat fresh, green grass in the spring.

Roundup at Konza Prairie

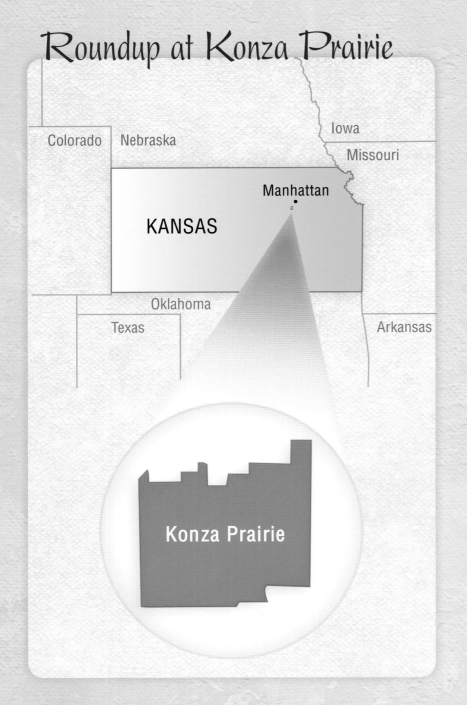

Colorado Nebraska

Iowa

Missouri

KANSAS

Manhattan

Oklahoma

Texas

Arkansas

Konza Prairie

The day of the bison roundup came. The roundup at Konza Prairie happens just once a year, at the end of October. Gene and his crew helped bring the bison to the corral. Veterinarians checked the health of the bison and gave them vaccinations to help protect them from diseases. It is during roundup that the new calves get their own ear tags.

Every bison on Konza Prairie has ear tags. The numbered tags tell Gene two things—what year the animal was born and who the animal is. Because each individual bison has its own special number, the ear tags help him keep track of the history of the herd.

Corral Design

Bison are a herd animal. They are uncomfortable being alone and feel much more secure with other members of their herd. The Konza Prairie bison corral was designed with this idea in mind, so the bison don't get frightened and hurt themselves. The corral allows the bison to see other animals in their herd but not the people working. The alleyways are narrow and curved, which makes the bison feel secure while gently encouraging them to move forward toward the scale and chute. Bison enter a squeeze chute to get their ear tags and vaccinations. The squeezing calms them down and makes it safe for the animals to be worked on. The process moves quickly: the entire herd of 300 to 400 animals is weighed and vaccinated in one day!

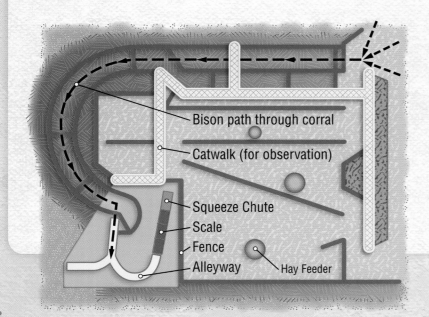

Bison path through corral

Catwalk (for observation)

Squeeze Chute

Scale

Fence

Alleyway Hay Feeder

Gene was especially careful with the little calf. The bison don't like to be put in tight places like a corral. They can get so nervous that they can hurt themselves. A nervous bison is a dangerous bison. Our little calf would have to be especially careful not to get stepped on by a scared adult.

Gene made sure the little calf wasn't too close to a bull or a big group of nervous bison. The autumn calf stayed with her mother and quickly moved through the chutes.

Migration

Some animals respond to changes in the weather by migrating, or moving from one area to another to find more favorable food or shelter. Killdeer and upland sandpipers are two birds that migrate to Konza Prairie in the spring. The killdeer typically winter in Mexico or Central America. They are one of the first arrivals to the prairie in early March. In fact, the first call of the killdeer is the sign that spring is coming. The upland sandpiper typically arrives a month later. Although most of the killdeer move on to other places, many of the upland sandpipers stick around, and there are usually many pairs of nesting birds at Konza Prairie. These migrants head south in the autumn, typically by September.

When it was the calf's turn to be weighed, all activity stopped. Everyone waited to hear. Gene yelled out, "197 pounds!"

She wasn't 200 pounds, but she was close! She might be able to survive the winter if her mother could take good care of her.

Loss of Tallgrass Prairie

The steel plow was invented by John Deere in 1837, specifically to break up the thick, root-filled sod of the prairie and replace native grasses with new kinds of grass: corn and wheat. When the native plants were plowed under, the animals that were dependent on prairie grasses, like the prairie chicken and American bison, began to disappear. At Konza Prairie, you can still see what a healthy tallgrass prairie looks like, including the plants and animals that call the prairie "home."

The little calf got her orange ear tags. Everyone now recognized her as #237. The orange ear tags were given to bison born between 2010 and 2019. The "2" at the beginning of the number told that this bison was born in 2012. The "37" meant that she was the thirty-seventh calf to go through the chute and get new tags.

Jill no longer had to guess who she was looking at. The ear tags made it much easier to identify all the different bison.

Predators

All natural systems include lots of different plants and animals. At the top of the food chain are the predators, which eat other animals. Examples of common prairie predators include owls, hawks, snakes, bobcats, coyotes, and wolves. Predators are often misunderstood and thought of as the bad guys when, in fact, they play an important role in a healthy ecosystem. Predators help keep the numbers of other animals down to prevent overpopulation and overgrazing. Coyotes are one of the most common predators on the prairie. Coyotes will eat just about anything, not only other animals but also fruit, grass, and dead things. If you ever get a chance to spend the night on a prairie, you'll probably hear the lonesome howls of coyotes as they communicate with their pack.

The little calf was safely released back to the prairie along with her mother and the other bison. It was a beautiful autumn day, and everyone at Konza Prairie hoped the good weather would last as long as possible.

Slowly, autumn changed
into winter. The days were cold,
and food was scarce. The bison calf was
in danger, not only of freezing, but also of
starvation or being hunted by coyotes. Luckily,
the little calf had an old, wise mother who had
been through many winters. She knew how to save
her energy by avoiding the cold wind and lying
down in the valleys. She preserved her strength
and was able to provide warm, nutritious milk
for her growing calf. And she was big
enough to protect the little calf from
being attacked by coyotes.

Phenology

The prairie has four distinct seasons: winter, spring, summer, and autumn. Weather determines how prairie plants and animals respond, something scientists are especially interested in. For example, the date when a flower blooms for the first time is important and might change by as much as a few weeks from year to year, depending on the weather. The study of the timing of "firsts" in an environment is called phenology. Some other firsts include the first bison calf of the year and the first day in early spring that we hear the call of the killdeer. Scientists record these plant and animal firsts on Konza Prairie and use that information to understand prairie life better.

Dates of Blooming on the Tallgrass Prairie

	March	April	May	June	July	August	September
Ground Plum	▓						
Plains Larkspur		▓	▓				
Butterfly Milkweed				▓			
Lead Plant					▓		
Blue Sage						▓	
Maximilian Sunflower							▓

The bison at Konza Prairie are able to freely wander inside a big 2,500-acre fenced enclosure. They can go down into valleys, where it is hard for people to see them. Because of this, Jill and Gene lost sight of the little calf. The last time they saw her was in December. She was with her mother and a group of other bison cows and calves.

They hoped she was growing and getting stronger. If she made it until spring, then her chance of survival was much higher.

Killdeer

Killdeer are birds with a funny name and a funny lifestyle. Their name comes from their distinctive call, which someone imagined sounds like a person yelling, "Kill deer, kill deer." Killdeer run along the edge of grass and gravel and make their nests in a slight depression, or dent in the ground. People have to watch carefully so they don't destroy killdeer nests by walking or driving on them.

One of the first signs of spring on the prairie is the return of the killdeer. Killdeer are birds with boldly striped feathers, long, thin legs, and a distinctive call that sounds like they're saying, "Kill deer, kill deer, kill deer!"

When Jill heard the first killdeer of the spring, she knew that if the little calf was still alive, she had survived the winter. The question was, had the little calf made it?

One month went by, and no one had seen the calf. The calf's mother had not been seen either, so everyone hoped the two were hiding somewhere together.

Fire on the Prairie

Fire is very important to the health of the prairie. Long ago, wildfires probably burned the prairie every three to four years. When there is no fire, a prairie will naturally turn into a shrubland, and years later, a forest. Grasses thrive when burned regularly because most of the grasses' structure is under the soil. Fires remove the old, dead leaves and allow rain and the warmth of the sun to reach the soil. Fire also keeps shrubs and trees from growing, so all of the soil's water and nutrients can go to the prairie plants rather than to invading shrubs or trees. Prairie managers carefully burn the prairie to keep the grasses and wildflowers healthy.

In the meantime, it was spring and time to get ready for burning. Burning the prairie removes the old, dead grass from past summers. Fire helps slow the growth of shrubs and trees that would take over a prairie if given the opportunity. By removing the cover of old grass, the soil is warmed by the rays of the sun. Rain can get to the soil faster without old plants being in the way. The soil gets warm and moist, and the roots begin to grow and send up new shoots into the spring air. Burning also releases nutrients back into the ground. The plants that grow after a fire are deep green and very nutritious. The bison love them!

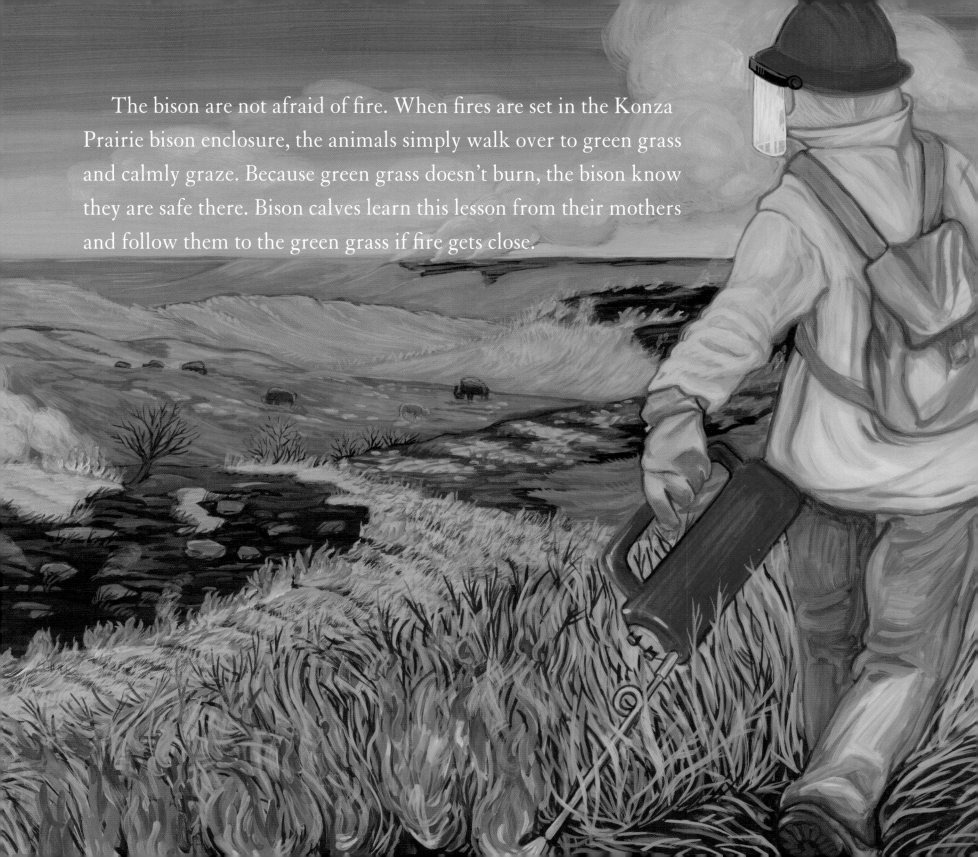

The bison are not afraid of fire. When fires are set in the Konza Prairie bison enclosure, the animals simply walk over to green grass and calmly graze. Because green grass doesn't burn, the bison know they are safe there. Bison calves learn this lesson from their mothers and follow them to the green grass if fire gets close.

After the bison area was burned, Jill watched the herd calmly move on to green grass. As she was watching, she thought she saw a small calf that might be #237. She ran and got her binoculars and took a good look. Yes! It was #237!

The little calf was there watching her, alive, healthy, and calmly eating. Gene guessed she had gained about 10 pounds over the winter, and was now rapidly gaining even more weight.

The little calf was a lucky calf. She had survived a long, cold winter and was well on her way to becoming a healthy, full-grown bison.

That same week the upland sandpipers returned. They had come back to the prairie to nest and raise their babies. The cycle of life on the prairie began again.

AUTHOR **Jill Haukos** has lived on the prairie her whole life, starting in South Dakota and then moving to west Texas and then finally, the Flint Hills of Kansas. Jill is the Director of Education at the Konza Prairie Biological Station. It is her job to provide prairie-based scientific experiences to area school children and to lead the training of volunteer docents. She and her husband, Dave, have one daughter, Katie, and they all enjoy life on the prairie.

ILLUSTRATOR **Joyce Mihran Turley** specializes in presenting images of nature with a painterly style and colorful palette, engaging readers of all ages. Having studied engineering along with fine art, Joyce's technical perspective results in images with a unique balance of analytic and artistic elements. Raised in upstate New York, Joyce has lived with her husband in the foothills of the Colorado Rockies for over 35 years. Her studio, located in their now "empty nest," permits convenient observation of raptors, deer, lizards, and snakes—just outside the picture windows!